I0539325

QUANTUM ADVENTURES IN SPARKSVILLE

STORIES ABOUT THE QUANTUM WORLD FOR KIDS

AMIL IMANI

COPYRIGHT @ 2024
AMIL IMANI

All rights reserved. No part of this book may be reproduced, stored in a retrieval system, or transmitted in any form or by any means, electronic, mechanical, photocopying, recording, or otherwise, without the prior written permission of the publisher, except for brief quotations embodied in critical reviews and certain other noncommercial uses permitted by copyright law.

For permissions, please contact:

Amil Imani
www.amilimani.us

TABLE OF CONTENTS

1

THE WONDER OF SPARKSVILLE

Sparksville, kids, ain't your ordinary town. For sure, you will notice its distinctive charm.

Here the meadows got that sparkle, like sprinkled magic dust. And the air?

It's always alive with the wonders of the night sky that you might have noticed right above your heads as you peek out your home windows.

Now, let's talk about the paths in Sparksville – Ah, well! They develop into gateways for adventures.

Consider strolling down a path, and abruptly, whoosh!

A secret passage appears out of thin air.

You could make it appear by the power of your mind whenever you want.

You see Sparksville is up in the sky, but not in any particular spot or time.

It's like a combination of
cool things from the future and
echoes from the distant past.

To make it real before you, all
you need is to be without a
doubt.

Just genuinely consider it, as
intensely as you can - one has to
kind of channel one's thoughts
with an intensity that rivals the
birth of stars.

The humans,
shall we say, or
the beings in
Sparksville are
one-of-a-kind –
they may now be
not quite like
us, more like
otherworldly
beings.

Though they may
seem to be like
human beings,
just like us!

When you consider going there, it's like watching a wonderful film.

But here's the intricate element – the humans in Sparksville don't know you're watching.

It is like you're a secret viewer and that they just go about their daily routine in Sparksville, doing cool and magical things.

One can only wonder what kind of cool and magical things they might be up to.

The possibilities are simply endless in a surreal place like Sparksville.

Although Sparksville comes from your imagination, you cannot control it once it manifests.

It's like your own creativity made a whole world but with a mind of its very own. It is a mixture of make-believe and real stuff, an area wherein vintage and the new exist together.

As you watch the mystical beings in Sparksville going about doing their thing, you are like a quiet observer in a front-row seat of a fantastic show.

Sparksville is a groovy adventure born from your imagination.

However, it turns into a real arena, which makes it so unique and mysterious out there among the clouds in the blue sky.

It's like having a treasure map wherein 'X' marks the spot, but you never know when that spot will appear or where it may be.

Simply put, you never really know what is coming.

Sparksville's magic plays by its own rules. Can't quite put your finger on it yet, can ya?

So, there you have it, kiddos – Sparksville is a city full of wonders that wreck all the rules of the games you have ever known.

Get ready for a wild journey in Sparksville!

2

MAKING
FRIENDS
WITH
QUANTUM
CREATURES

This wild, fascinating story
will keep you on your toes and
make everything exciting!

So alright, young fellas, gather
'round' for an excellent
adventure story about
Sparksville's unstoppable duo -
Zoom and Zap.

These inseparable
buddies are always
up for any
interesting
challenge!

Their friendship? In
perspective, it is not
your typical, run-of-
the-mill, usual kind.

It is, if you please, out of the
world.

Zoom and Zap share an
extraordinary connection as if
they're one entangled species.

You know how the celestial beings in the night sky twinkle and communicate with each other without the need to speak? Just natural magic!

Picture communicating with your friend without uttering a single syllable.

It truly is the enigmatic bond Zoom and Zap thrive in, comparable to the radiant illumination in Sparksville.

Let's dig into their captivating journey into the quantum realm, where their unique friendship takes a prominent stage!

Our story unfolds with those two inseparable pals, ceaselessly entangled in each other's organization.

 So, buckle up, kids, for a quantum adventure like no other!

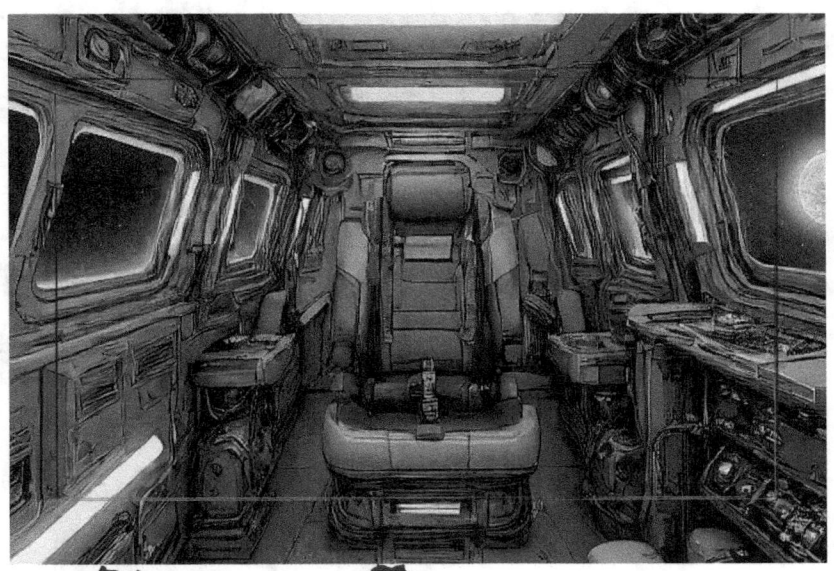

It was a superb, sunny day, with a bright solar portrayal on the meadows with golden colors.

Zoom and Zap, in their usual **15**
spontaneous fashion, set forth on
a captivating adventure!

It all begins after
they come upon a
mysterious door in a
meadow hidden
between historic
bushes.

A weird symbol
catches Zoom's eye,
and he exclaims,
"Zap, look at this!"

They push that mysterious door,
and bam, it swings open,
revealing a luminous vortex.

This vortex, twirling with bursts
of color, beckons them with
whispers of the extraordinary.

Without hesitation, Zoom and Zap step into the swirling brilliance, moving into the unknown and an unseen world.

It's a journey painted with marvels past their wildest imagination, just like the political weather we are all familiar with – you just can't predict, folks, for it is wild, truly fantastic!

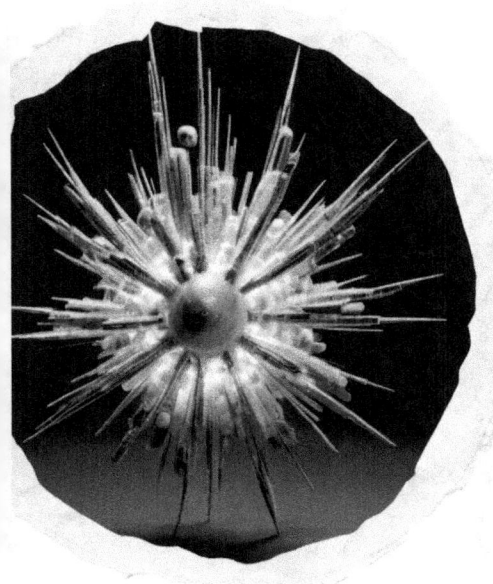

Alright, kiddos, brace yourself for the adventures of our entangled friends Zoom and Zap in this new mesmerizing world – it is a hoot, I promise!

Soon, our friends Zoom and Zap get to meet some quirky characters.

There's Quark, a particle buzzing with energy (imagine a bumblebee, however tinier);

Photon, who is like a sparkly dancer with a costume made of fairy lighting fixtures;

and Neutron, a massive with a magnetic persona (he's now not a fridge magnet, but he's just as cool).

The quantum creatures, who were a bit mysterious to begin with, soon became friends with Zoom and Zap.

They indulged in a lot of games and exciting activities as they raced with Quark to understand his mysterious ways and moves, similar to a bumblebee humming about, now here, now there.

Quark is a little quantum racer, zipping and zooming in unpredictable ways.

By racing with him, Zoom and Zap discovered that things may be super unpredictable in the quantum realm, much like Quark's speedy maneuvers!

It's like seeking to capture a hummingbird – you by no means understand where it would go next!

Such was the sense of wonder, mystery, and unpredictability that our friends encountered in the quantum realm.

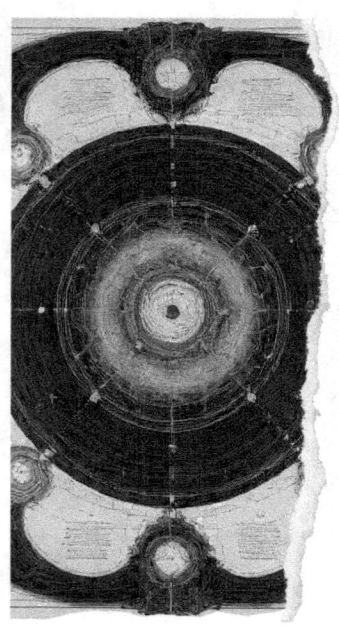

Zoom and Zap realised the need for a different set of rules and tools to navigate and understand this unique and enigmatic domain presented to them in these quantum realms.

They sat back and enjoyed captivating light displays with Photon.

Those displays were like magical dance performances where lights sparkled and shimmered in fantastic patterns.

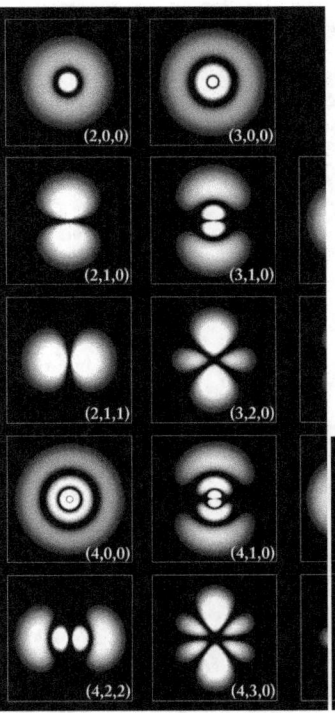

Such was the graceful and ethereal dancing, with intricate light patterns, shimmering choreography and dazzling movements.

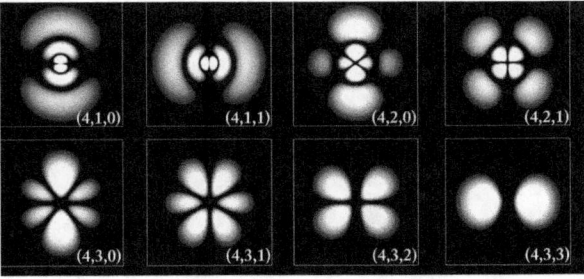

It was Photon who revealed the enchanting art of superposition. Our friends realized that Photon's captivating light dance was actually superposition in action!

They could be in multiple places all at once.

Next, they even felt the giant bear hug of Neutron's magnetic persona. Our team Zoom and Zap became unstoppable!

Many secrets of their own enchanting world were revealed in this short period.

It was a very fulfilling experience for both.

3

SOLVING PUZZLES: KEY TO WAY BACK HOME

Zoom and Zap felt excitement **23** pulsing as they discovered that these quantum creatures held the key to their journey home.

But, as with every journey of adventure, there were challenges to be overcome.

The route home was intricately tied to puzzles that lay ahead, relying on the mind-bending principles of quantum mechanics.

They need to solve these quantum puzzles to unlock the way out of the quantum realm.

Their first challenge was through an intricate maze based on quantum entanglement.

It was a unique kind of maze. They had to guide the particles via interwoven paths, ensuring they remained connected. Instead of walls and doors, this maze had tracks that were connected specially.

And there was a twist, too!

When two particles were on different paths, they became "entangled." And herein lay the secret to solving the journey through this maze.

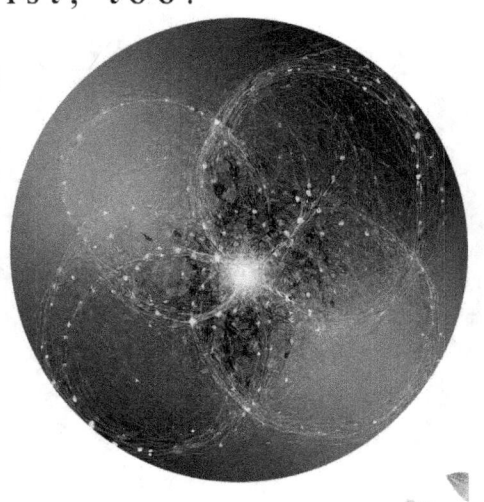

Their first challenge was through an intricate maze based on quantum entanglement.

Since they were entangled, whatever happened to one particle would immediately affect the other, no matter how far apart they were.

Thus, our friends only had to be cared for in every pair. It was easier than it seemed once they realized the concept behind the puzzle.

So, Zoom and Zap had to plan their moves carefully. They had to find the entangled pairs, which was the tricky part.

It required careful planning,
understanding how entanglement
worked, and using that knowledge
to navigate the maze
successfully.

They had to
resort to quick
trial and error
to establish the
pairs.

To solve the
challenge, Zoom
and Zap had to
think ahead and
consider how
their actions
would impact
the entangled
particles. They
also had to find
the right path
combinations to
connect the
particles
throughout the
maze.

Then, all they needed to do to
make the entangled particles
come out of the maze was to
guide one in each pair carefully.
Since they always stayed
connected, even if they took
different paths, the teams would
pop out at the same time.

It was like
holding hands
with someone
throughout
and ensuring
you stayed
together in
the maze no
matter where
you went.

Thus, when one comes out, you
pull out the other long!

Our friends
probably used
the principle of
"spooky action
at a distance"
to effectively
guide just one
particle out.

So, the first challenge was guiding the entangled particles through the interwoven paths, knowing they were always connected.

Zoom and Zap showed their cleverness and problem-solving skills by completing this challenge.

They learned about the fascinating concept of entanglement, where particles can be connected uniquely, almost like they have a secret communication channel.

As they triumphantly completed this challenge, our intrepid friends learned that particles can be entangled.

Thus, changing the state of one instantly affects the other, no matter the distance between them.

It was like magic, but it involved particles dancing in unison across the quantum maze instead of wands.

Our friends were beginning to realize that there is a more fundamental kind of magic at work in the universe, one that is based on the laws of the Universe.

These puzzles helped our friends to understand that it was not about illusion or trickery, but about understanding the world around us and our place in it.

4

ZOOM AND ZAP GET NEARER TO HOME

Well, little folks, strap yourselves in because Zoom and Zap, those two quantum adventurers, are now about to dive headfirst into a puzzle of superposition! They have to get back home, you know!

So picture this: they gotta manipulate and arrange quantum objects in a way that lets them exist, all at once, in more places than you've got fingers on both hands.

It's like arranging toys on a shelf, but instead of being in just one place, they could be in multiple locations at once!

Now, that's what I call a quantum riddle! Do you get it?

Ok, pay attention to this, kids. In the quantum realm, things can get a bit wacky.

Unlike our everyday world, where things stick to one spot, quantum objects can pull off a magic trick – they can exist in many places all at the same time.

It's like magic, but instead of pulling rabbits out of hats, we're talking about particles dancing around like there's no tomorrow!

So kids, know that the energetic motion of particles in the quantum realms is the true magic of the unseen world of quantum reality, where particles behave in ways that seem to defy our understanding.

That's how things are, and
things work in the Quantum
world.

Zoom and Zap, those dynamic
pals, didn't shy away from the
challenge. They put their
incredible teamwork to the test,
mixed in a bit of trial and error,
and voila!

They discovered the right
combinations that simultaneously
made quantum objects exist in
multiple states.

It was like they were putting on
a dance show for their quantum
friends, making them twirl and
spin in different places all at
once!

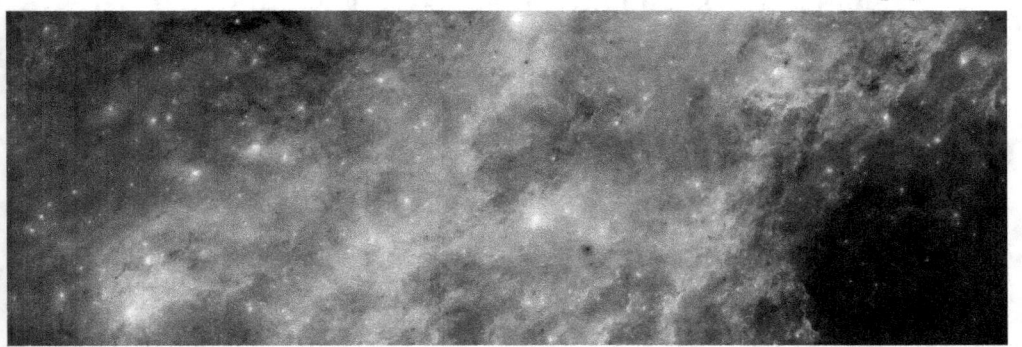

Now, hold on tight because each challenge brought Zoom and Zap closer to unraveling the mysteries of the quantum realm.

They learned about wave-particle duality – when objects behave as waves and particles.

It might sound mind-boggling,
but trust me, it's fascinating
stuff! The quantum world was
full of surprises and wonders
that made their understanding of
the universe more significant and
better than ever!

And as they
got past each
puzzle, Zoom
and Zap were
not only on a
rollercoaster
of discovery;
they were
getting
nearer to
home!

Their journey wasn't just about
solving puzzles but also about
making friends.

Zoom and Zap had a grand time
with the quirky quantum
creatures - laughing, playing
games, and marveling at the
wonders of the quantum realm.

The more challenges they conquered, the more they realized that the quantum playground is full of surprises, and the more it expanded their understanding of the universe like never before.

So, with every triumph, Zoom and Zap felt the magic of quantum concepts come to life.

The puzzles they solved were like secret codes that unlocked the mysteries of the quantum realm, revealing an enchanting world where the ordinary became extraordinary.

As they continued their quantum adventure, our dynamic duo couldn't help but be grateful to their quantum friends for the incredible journey that turned learning into a playful and exciting experience!

And more than all, they had to return home to their family and friends!

5

THE FINAL
HURDLE

Zoom and Zap grew restless,
feeling a strong urge to return
home. There was no end to the
puzzles they had to solve to
return home.

Zoom sighed,
"Zap, we've
got to find a
way back
home. These
puzzles never
seem to end!"

Zap, looking
determined,
responded,
"Don't worry,
Zoom. We'll
figure it out.
We always
do!"

As they searched for clues, Zoom
exclaimed,

"The quantum creatures are gone!
And our way home is closed.
What are we going to do?"

Zap, with a hint of optimism, said, "Maybe Lumina, the Quantum kid from our own world, can help. She always knows something interesting."

Just as they spoke, Lumina appeared, a twinkle in her eyes. "Having trouble, Zoom and Zap?"

Zoom, surprised, asked, "Lumina, what are you doing here? And how did you get here? This is supposed to be a place of swirling mysteries and quantum wonders!"

Lumina chuckled, "Ah, Quantum entanglement brought me here. I sensed you two needed a hand."

Zap, relieved, grinned,
"Well, we could use all
the help we can get
These puzzles are
getting trickier!

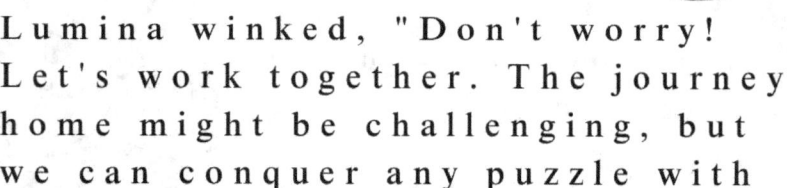

Moreover, those
quantum creatures
helping us have
vanished without a
trace."

Lumina winked, "Don't worry!
Let's work together. The journey
home might be challenging, but
we can conquer any puzzle with
teamwork!"

Lumina
guided Zoom
and Zap into
the
mysterious
room, where
an ethereal
glow bathed
everything
in a magical
light.

The air hummed with energy,
and mesmerizing quantum objects
at the room's center floated
gracefully, defying the laws of
nature.

"This room
holds the key
to a quantum
adventure
beyond
reality,"
Lumina
explained, her
eyes sparkling
excitedly.

Zoom and Zap stared in awe at
the quantum objects.

Lumina continued,
"These objects exist in
more than one state at
the same time, a
fascinating phenomenon
called 'superposition.'
Now, your task is to
unravel the secrets of
arranging them to keep
their multi-state
existence intact."

The room
itself seemed
like a puzzle
waiting to be
solved, and
Zoom couldn't
help but ask,
"But how do
we even begin
Lumina?"

Lumina grinned, "Think of it like
putting together a puzzle.
Instead of fitting pieces in a
specific way, you must find
combinations that allow these
objects to be simultaneously in
many states."

Zoom and Zap
exchanged determined
glances and started
experimenting.

They moved the
quantum objects
around, discovering
that they blended and overlapped
when placed close, creating a
beautiful mix of possibilities.

"Look at this!" Zoom exclaimed as he placed an object high up. It was simultaneously both big and small.

It was, indeed, a paradox – an intricately carved cylindrical object no bigger than his palm, yet its intricate geometric patterns seemed to stretch on endlessly, into the universe

"It's...impossible," Zoom breathed, mesmerized.

The air crackled with a strange energy, and the object hummed softly, vibrating against his skin.

Equally excited, Zap placed an object near a particular crystal, and it turned red and blue simultaneously.

Lumina nodded approvingly,
"You're getting the hang of it!"

Through trial and error, the trio
uncovered the right
combinations, marveling at how
different arrangements affected
the superposition of the quantum
objects.

Each step brought them closer to
unlocking the room's secrets.

Zoom and Zap realized they had cracked the puzzle as they successfully arranged the quantum objects in superposition. With a proud smile, Lumina said, "Now, for the final challenge."

The explorers carefully observed and analyzed the behavior of each quantum object, using their knowledge of superposition, entanglement, and other quantum principles gained during their adventure.

Placing the objects in a sequence that reflected their understanding of quantum mechanics, Zoom and Zap activated the final puzzle.

A surge of brilliant light erupted from the arrangement, forming a glowing vortex before their eyes.

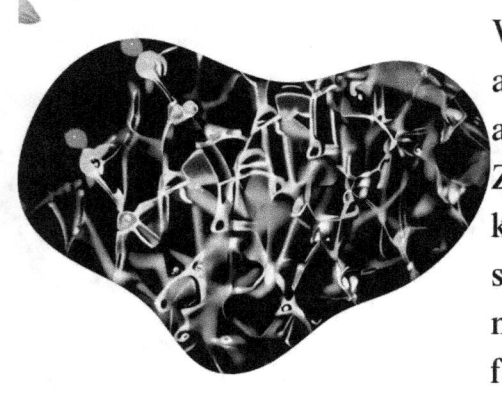

With a sense of **47**
accomplishment
and excitement,
Zoom and Zap
knew they had
successfully
navigated the
final hurdle.

The vortex stood as a radiant
gateway, ready to transport them
back to their own world.

The duo stepped into the
shimmering light, eager to return
home, their quantum adventure
reaching a thrilling conclusion.

As they crossed the
threshold, the familiar
sting of reality washed
over them. Gone were
the swirling nebulas and
impossible landscapes,
replaced by the
reassuring solidity of
their home.

SUPPLEMENTARY READING
1

Zoom and Zap's appreciation for the wonders of quantum mechanics.

Mind-Expanding Possibilities:

Zoom and Zap saw how particles can exist in multiple states at once, how When two particles become entangled, they remain connected no matter how far apart they are, and how the tiniest particles could have a significant impact on the larger, macroscopic world.

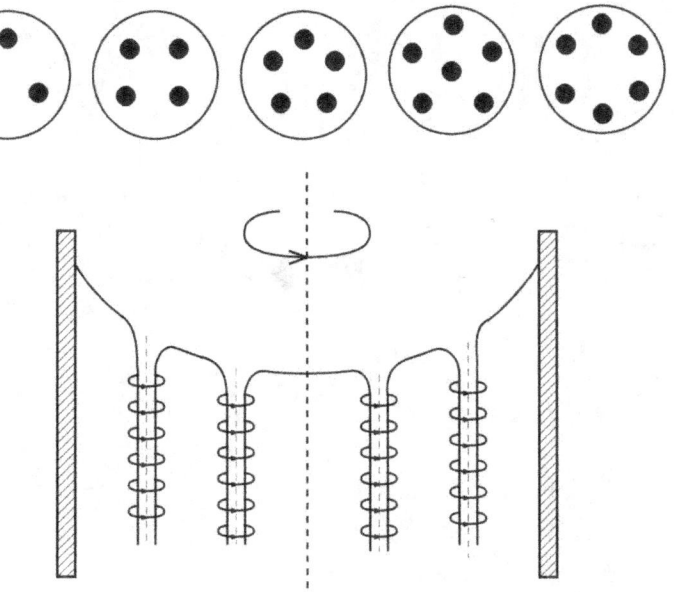

Through their adventures, Zoom and Zap learned that the act of observation or measurement can influence the behavior of quantum particles.

They realized that this concept has broader implications beyond quantum mechanics and can be applied to various aspects of life. They understood how observation could distort any perception of reality and how our own behavior may change when we know we are being watched.

SUPPLEMENTARY READING
2

type of questions that will arise in your mind

How can something be big and small, or red and blue, at the same time? It doesn't make sense!

Can we see examples of superposition in our everyday lives, or is it only for tiny particles?

Can we create or observe superposition ourselves, or is it something only scientists can do?

What other strange things can happen in the quantum realm? Are there more examples like superposition?

Can we use superposition for anything practical or useful in our daily lives?

Does superposition apply to living things, like plants, animals, or people, or is it only for non-living particles?

Are there any real-world applications or technologies that use the principles of superposition?

Here are a couple of examples how:

Lasers: Superposition helps focus the light inside a laser, making it super bright and precise.

Superconducting magnets: These powerful magnets used in trains and medical equipment rely on the unique properties of electrons in a "superposed" state.

6

MYSTERY OF THE VANISHING OBJECTS

The quiet town of Sparksville was enveloped in a peculiar mystery that left everyone perplexed. Determined to uncover the truth, our friends Zoom, Zap, Quarky, and Photonix embarked on a mission to get to the bottom of it.

So what was this little mystery they wanted to solve. It was just that objects in their town had started vanishing and reappearing in different locations.

The determination of the four friends knew no bounds, and very soon they eagerly banded together as the ingenious Quantum Detectives.

One sunny morning, the friends gathered at their secret headquarters, a treehouse hidden deep in the woods

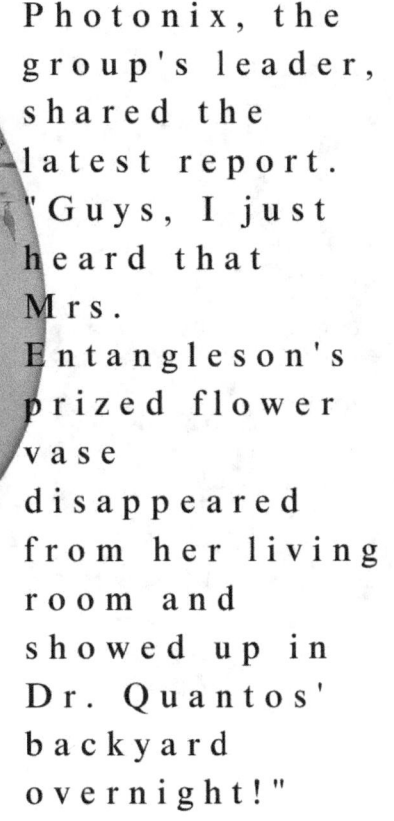

Photonix, the group's leader, shared the latest report. "Guys, I just heard that Mrs. Entangleson's prized flower vase disappeared from her living room and showed up in Dr. Quantos' backyard overnight!"

Zoom gasped in disbelief.
"That's impossible! Objects can't
mysteriously teleport themselves
like that!"

Zap nodded, scratching his head.
"It's like they're playing their
own version of hide-and-seek."

Quarky, the
tech-savvy
member of the
team, pulled
out her tablet
with excitement
in her eyes.

"You know
what, guys? I've
been delving
into the depths
of scientific
mysteries, and I
stumbled upon a
fascinating
realm known as
'Cosmic
Enigmas.'

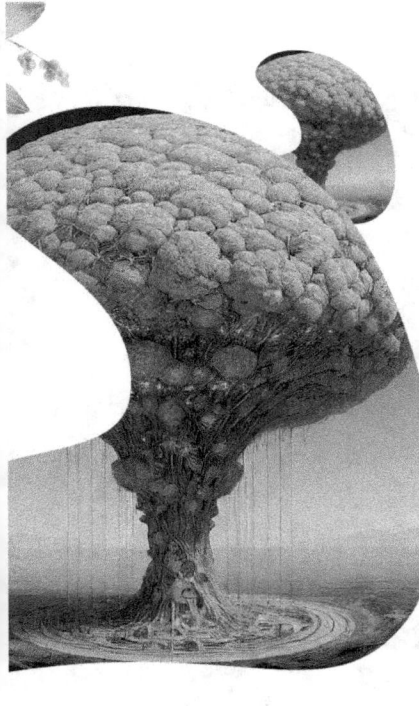

It's a mind-bending domain that explores the peculiar phenomena that occur beyond our understanding of the universe."

Photonix looked at Quarky with a mix of intrigue and excitement.

"Cosmic Enigmas, huh? That sounds like a fascinating realm explore to solve this mystery.

What exactly did you find about celestial paradoxes, astral anomalies, and cosmic conundrums?"

Zoom gasped in disbelief. "That's impossible! Objects can't mysteriously teleport themselves like that!"

Zap nodded, scratching his head. "It's like they're playing their own version of hide-and-seek."

Quarky, the tech-savvy member of the team, pulled out her tablet with excitement in her eyes.

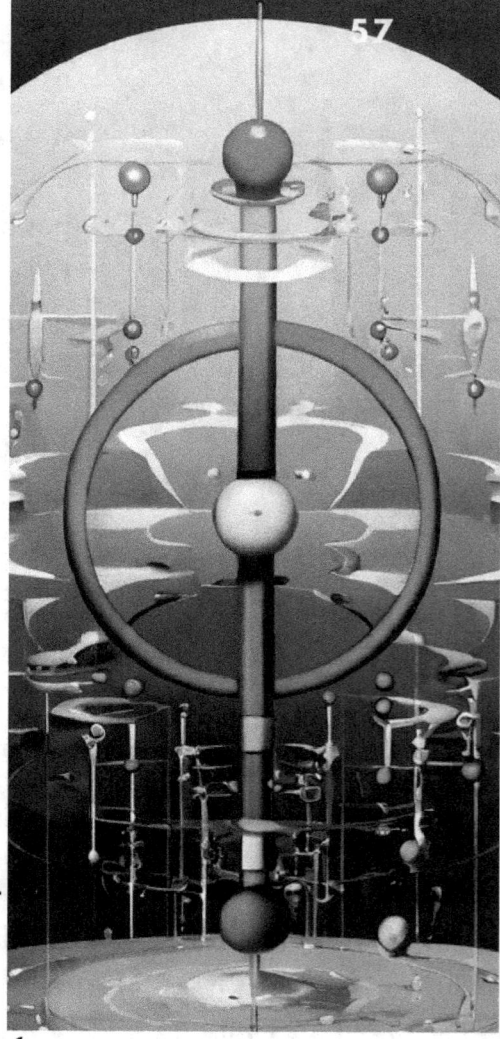

"You know what, guys? I've been delving into the depths of scientif mysteries, and I stumbled upon a fascinating realm known as 'Cosmic Enigmas.'

It's a mind-bending domain that explores the peculiar phenomena that occur beyond our understanding of the universe."

Photonix looked at Quarky with a mix of intrigue and excitement."

Cosmic Enigmas, huh? That sounds like a fascinating realm to explore to solve this mystery. What exactly did you find about celestial paradoxes, astral anomalies, and cosmic conundrums?"

Quarky grinned, eager to share her newfound knowledge.

"Ah, where do I even begin?" Quarky exclaimed, her eyes sparkling with excitement.

"Well, Photonix, celestial paradoxes are these mind-bending situations where the behavior of celestial objects seems to defy our understanding of physics. It's like when you have a star that appears older than the universe itself! It challenges our fundamental assumptions."

Photonix's eyes widened with curiosity. "Wow! That's incredible! We have at least made a start, thanks to you Quarky."

Zoom quipped in, "Yes, we should be able to get to the root of all those sudden and strange occurrences here in Sparksville."

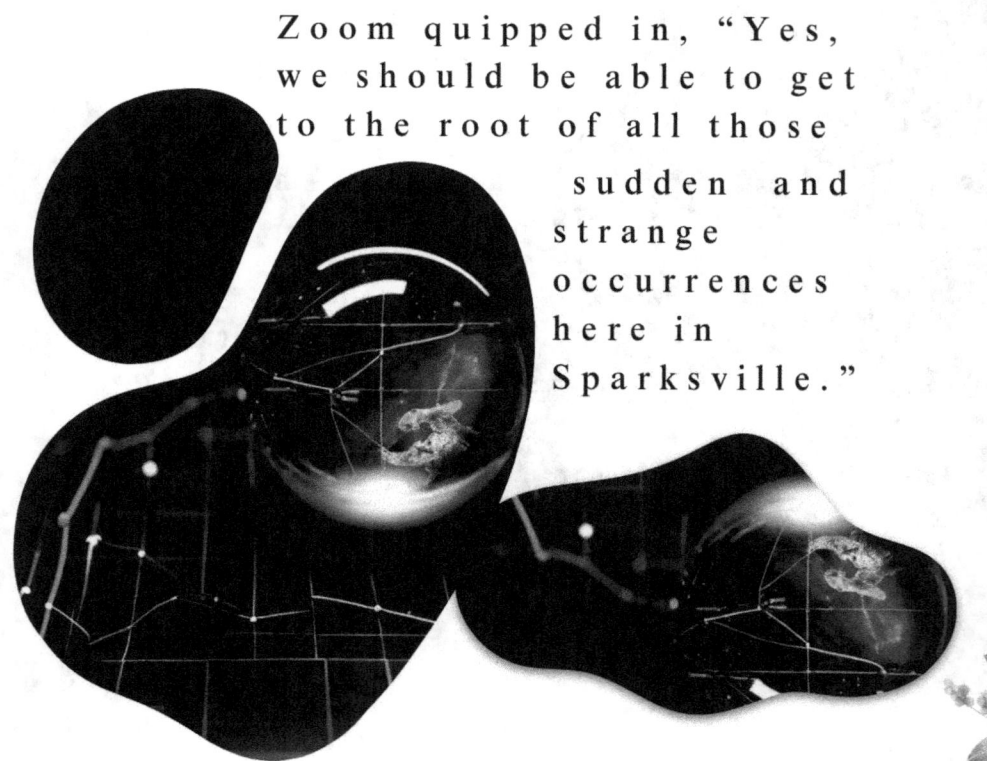

Quarky nodded enthusiastically. "Exactly! It would help explain how these objects behave in ways that completely defy our everyday experiences and logic!"

Intrigued, the friends gathered around Quarky as she explained the counterintuitive nature of the quantum world.

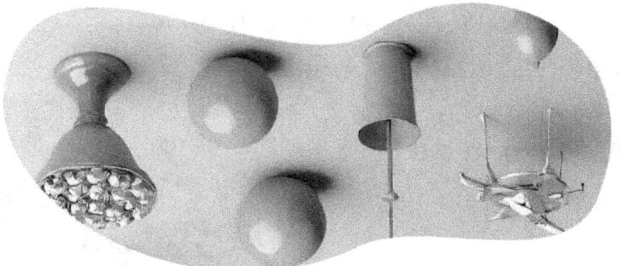

Quarky continued and she spoke of quantum tunneling, where particles can magically pass through solid barriers, and the observer effect, where simply observing a particle changes its behavior.

The friends perked up, their
eyes widening with curiosity.

Armed with this newfound
knowledge, the Quantum
Detectives began their
investigation.

Their first stop was
Mrs. Entangleson's
house. They carefully
examined the spot
where the vase had
vanished.

Zap noticed something peculiar.
"Look! There's a faint shimmer in
the air. It's like a doorway to
another dimension."

Zoom frowned.
"But how do we
open it?"

"Maybe it's like
Schrödinger's cat,"
Photonix chimed
in, "We have to
observe it to see
what happens."

Taking a deep breath, the friends collectively focused their gaze on the shimmer.

Suddenly, the doorway opened, revealing a mysterious room filled with swirling colors and strange contraptions.

The room was unlike anything they had ever seen before. The air crackled with energy, and the walls seemed to shift and morph as if they were alive.

Zap, Zoom, Quarky and Photonix cautiously stepped through the shimmering doorway, feeling a strange tingling sensation as they crossed the threshold.

As they entered the room, they were greeted by a chorus of soft, melodic chimes that simultaneously seemed to emanate from nowhere and everywhere.

The colors swirling around them danced in mesmerizing patterns, casting an otherworldly glow over the entire space.

Curious yet slightly apprehensive, their hearts pounding with excitement, the friends explored the mysterious room, seeing the strange contraptions that adorned the walls.

Some appeared to be intricate machines with gears and levers that moved independently, while others seemed to pulsate with an ethereal light.

"It's like the room is alive," Zoom remarked, their eyes wide with wonder.

They discovered a lab belonging to the brilliant yet reclusive scientist Dr. Quantos.

The air crackled with an electricity that wasn't entirely explainable, and cryptic symbols glowed on dusty beakers and consoles.

Dr. Quantos had been conducting groundbreaking experiments within his lab to harness the power of cosmic enigmas.

His work delved into the mysteries of the universe, seeking to unlock the secrets of dimensions beyond our own.

"It's like the room is alive," Zoom remarked, their eyes wide with wonder.

Dr. Quantos explained that his experiments had gone awry, causing objects in Sparkesville to behave erratically.

A hush fell over the group as Dr. Quantos, his eyes filled with a mixture of regret and manic excitement, launched into his explanation.

"It all started with..."
he began, his voice raspy from
disuse, "a simple attempt to
manipulate the fundamental
forces of nature. I sought to
understand the very fabric of
reality, to bend it to my will.
But alas," he threw his hands up
in despair, "my calculations were
flawed, my ambition outstripped
my understanding."

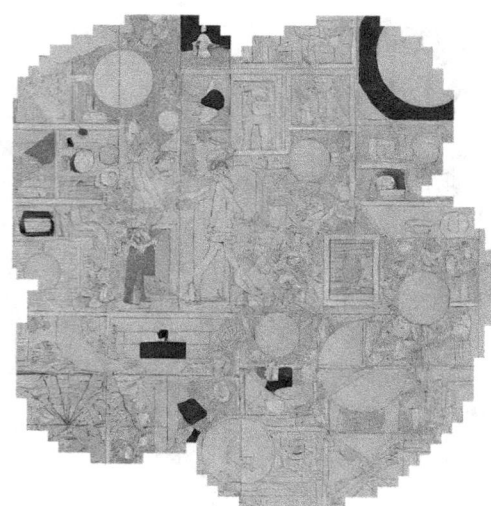

"I was trying to
push the
boundaries of
my current
understanding,
but I
unintentionally
disrupted the
fabric of
reality," he
confessed.

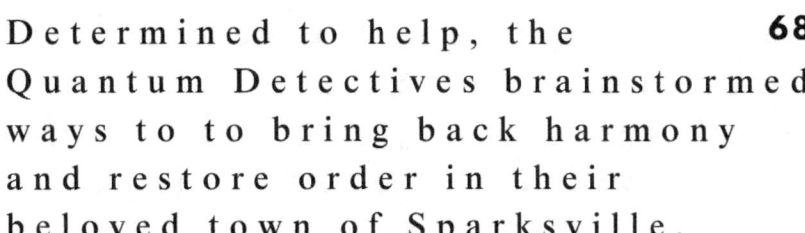

Determined to help, the
Quantum Detectives brainstormed
ways to to bring back harmony
and restore order in their
beloved town of Sparksville.

Zoom and Zap went out looking
for clues.

Photonix and Quarky sat down
together and brainstormed
strategies, leveraging their
understanding of quantum
tunneling and the principles of
cosmic enigmas.

Quarky suggested using their
knowledge of quantum tunneling
to guide the misplaced objects
back to their original locations.

Photonix nodded, "If we can track the quantum states of the misplaced objects and understand the energy barriers they encounter, we can guide them back to their original locations using the principles of quantum tunneling?"

Photonix devised a plan to build a device that could measure the observer effect and influence the behavior of the objects.

With teamwork and ingenuity, the Quantum Detectives set to work. They constructed the Observer-O-Meter, a gadget capable of observing and manipulating quantum particles.

Zap held the device while Zoom, Photonix, and Quarky scoured the town for the missing objects.

Using the Observer-O-Meter, they carefully observed each object and willed it to return to its rightful place.

They watched in awe as the objects vanished from their hands and reappeared where they belonged.

Finally, after hours of hard work, Sparksville was back to normal.

The friends bid farewell to Dr. Quantos, grateful for the knowledge and insights he had shared with them about the Cosmic Enigmas.

They promised to stay in touch and share their knowledge of quantum mechanics with him.

They never forgot their promise to Dr. Quantos and regularly arranged meetups together, where they shared their latest discoveries and insights.

Together, they pushed the boundaries of what was known, constantly seeking to unravel the deepest secrets of the universe.

Years passed, the initial shock of Dr. Quantos' experiments fading into a bittersweet memory.

Yet, Dr. Quantos, remained a guiding spirit. His cryptic messages, delivered through dusty robots or flickering holograms, sparked heated debates and continued to fuel research for age to come.

SUPPLEMENTARY READING
3

Type of questions that will arise in your (the kid reader's) mind

How do particles teleport or vanish according to the cosmic enigmas?

According to quantum mechanics, particles can exhibit behaviors like teleportation or vanishing due to phenomena such as quantum tunneling.

Quantum tunneling is when particles can pass through barriers, like walls or solid objects as if they can magically "tunnel" through them. This phenomenon arises from the probabilistic nature of particles at the quantum level.

Can we observe quantum tunneling in our everyday lives?

Quantum tunneling typically occurs on tiny scales, such as at the atomic and subatomic levels.

While we can't directly observe it in our everyday lives, scientists have conducted experiments demonstrating quantum tunneling in controlled laboratory settings.

Can we build gadgets like the Observer-O-Meter in real life?

Not exactly! But Our scientists and engineers are constantly pushing the boundaries of technology and developing new tools to study and manipulate quantum systems. quantum computers and quantum sensors, are active research areas and hold great potential for the future.

SUPPLEMENTARY READING
4
Explaining quantum portals and the phenomenon of quantum tunneling

A portal refers to a doorway, gateway, or entrance that provides a passage from one place to another.

It is often associated with a magical or extraordinary means of transportation, allowing individuals to move between different locations or dimensions.

In the context of the story, the shimmering doorway discovered by the Quantum Detectives can be considered a portal, as it serves as a passage between their world and the mysterious room belonging to Dr. Quantos.

Portals are commonly depicted in myths, legends, and fantasy literature as a fascinating plot device that adds an element of wonder and adventure to stories.

Have you ever imagined stepping into a magical doorway that takes you to a completely different place, like a hidden world or a secret room? Well, that's the idea behind a quantum portal!

It's a beautiful blend of science and fantasy, hinting at possibilities beyond our current understanding of the universe.

Can you imagine your own quantum portal? Where does it lead? What are the rules that govern its existence? Are there any dangers associated with using it?

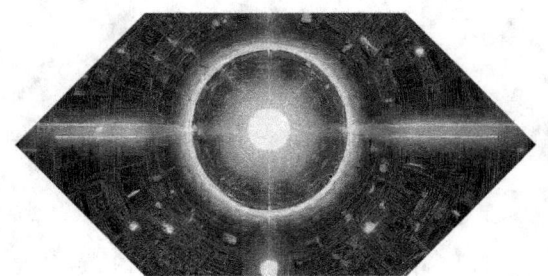

7
ENDLESS PARALLEL PAW-SIBILITIES

In the futuristic town of Sparksville, where the boundaries of reality blur, there resided a mischievous and inquisitive cat called Fluffy.

Fluffy was renowned for her knack of finding herself entangled in all manner of mischief, with her insatiable curiosity frequently whisking her away on the most extraordinary escapades.

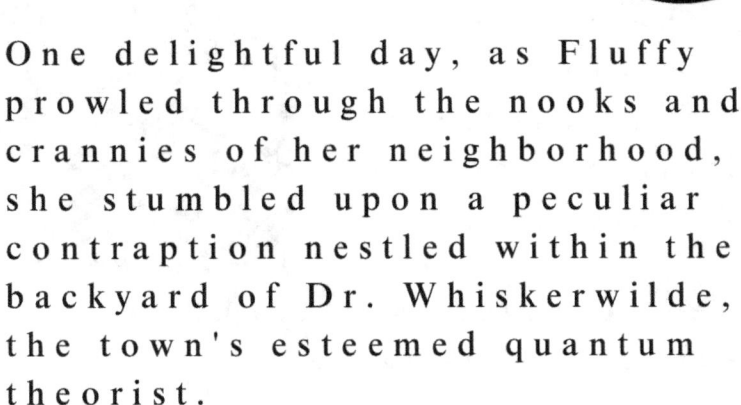

One delightful day, as Fluffy prowled through the nooks and crannies of her neighborhood, she stumbled upon a peculiar contraption nestled within the backyard of Dr. Whiskerwilde, the town's esteemed quantum theorist.

It was a shimmering, swirling
portal that seemed to beckon
Fluffy with its mysterious allure,
its hues of vibrant colors
dancing in the air like ethereal
ribbons.

Unable to resist
her feline
curiosity, Fluffy
mustered up all her
courage and leaped
into the swirling
portal, her heart
pounding with both
excitement and
trepidation.

To her surprise, she found
herself in a strange and
unfamiliar place.

Everything around her seemed different like she had entered a parallel world.

As Fluffy looked around, she noticed a gray-haired, bespectacled cat resembling her beloved Dr. Whiskerwilde back home.

Intrigued, Fluffy approached the professor, who seemed equally surprised to see her.

"Meow! Who are you? And where am I?" Fluffy asked, her whiskers twitching with excitement.

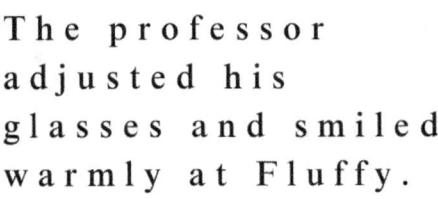

The professor adjusted his glasses and smiled warmly at Fluffy.

Fluffy listened intently as Professor Whiskerborrow began unraveling the mysteries of parallel universes.

He described how these universes existed alongside each other, each with its possibilities and outcomes.

"Well, you see, Fluffy, according to the theory of quantum multiverse, there are countless universes that exist simultaneously."

The professor continued, "Each universe comes with its possibilities. This portal you entered can transport you between these parallel worlds."

The professor shared an intriguing anecdote about a parallel universe where all cats had wings and ruled over the land.

Fluffy imagined soaring through the skies, her fluffy tail trailing behind her as she ruled over a kingdom of flying felines.

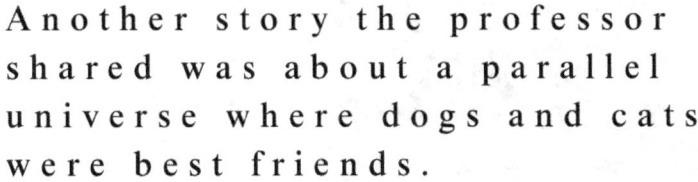

Another story the professor shared was about a parallel universe where dogs and cats were best friends.

They worked together to solve mysteries and save the world from evil masterminds.

Fluffy pictured herself as a detective, donning a Sherlock Holmes hat and carrying a magnifying glass, teaming up with a loyal canine companion to solve puzzling cases.

As Fluffy's excitement grew, she couldn't help but ask if there were any parallel universes where cats were the rulers of the human world.

The professor chuckled and shared a tale about a universe where humans served as loyal subjects to their feline overlords.

The cats lounged on velvet thrones while humans catered to their every need, from grooming to serving gourmet meals.

Fluffy imagined herself wearing a crown, sitting atop a regal throne, and being adored by humans who showered her affection and treats.

The professor's whiskers wiggled with amusement.

"Fear not, my dear Fluffy."

"I shall guide you on this extraordinary journey. To return home, we must find the correct portal that leads back to our universe. Each universe has its own unique signature, and we need to identify the one that matches yours."

Together, Fluffy and Professor Whiskerborrow ventured through one portal after another.

They always took care to return to the original Universe each time before entering the next portal.

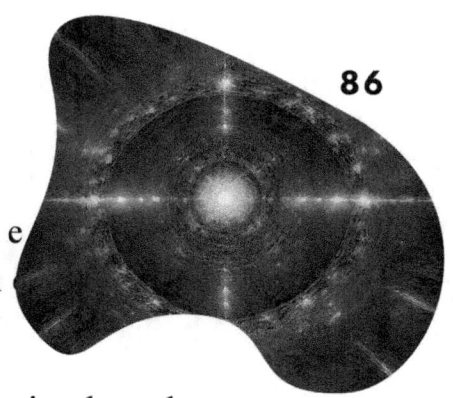

The professor was indeed a master of multiverse travel.

Together, they encountered all sorts of fascinating creatures along the way.

They met a three-headed dog who loved to play fetch, a group of musical birds that sang in perfect harmony, and even a gravity-defying squirrel that zipped through the trees.

As Fluffy and Professor **87**
Whiskerborrow embarked on their
journey through the parallel
universes, Professor Whiskers
took every opportunity to teach
Fluffy about the fascinating
concepts they encountered.

The paw-sibilities
were endless.

One day, they
arrived in a
universe where all
the colors were
inverted.

Fluffy blinked in
confusion as she
looked at the
bright blue grass
and the yellow sky
above.

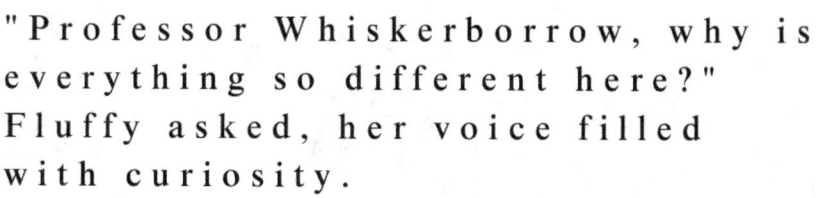

"Professor Whiskerborrow, why is
everything so different here?"
Fluffy asked, her voice filled
with curiosity.

The professor sat down next to
Fluffy and began to explain.

"Ah, my dear Fluffy, welcome to a parallel universe where the colors are inverted.

In this reality, what we perceive as blue appears red here, and vice versa."

Fluffy's eyes widened as she observed the unusual surroundings. "That's so strange! How does this happen?"

Professor Whiskerborrow stroked his chin thoughtfully.

"You see, Fluffy, in each parallel universe, the fundamental properties of the world can be slightly different.

"It's like having a different set of rules for how things work. In this universe, the color spectrum is flipped, creating a new way of perceiving the world."

Fluffy tilted her head, still trying to wrap her mind around the concept. "So, does that mean there are other universes where everything is even more different?"

The professor nodded, his whiskers twitching. "Absolutely, Fluffy! There are infinite parallel universes, each with its own unique set of possibilities."

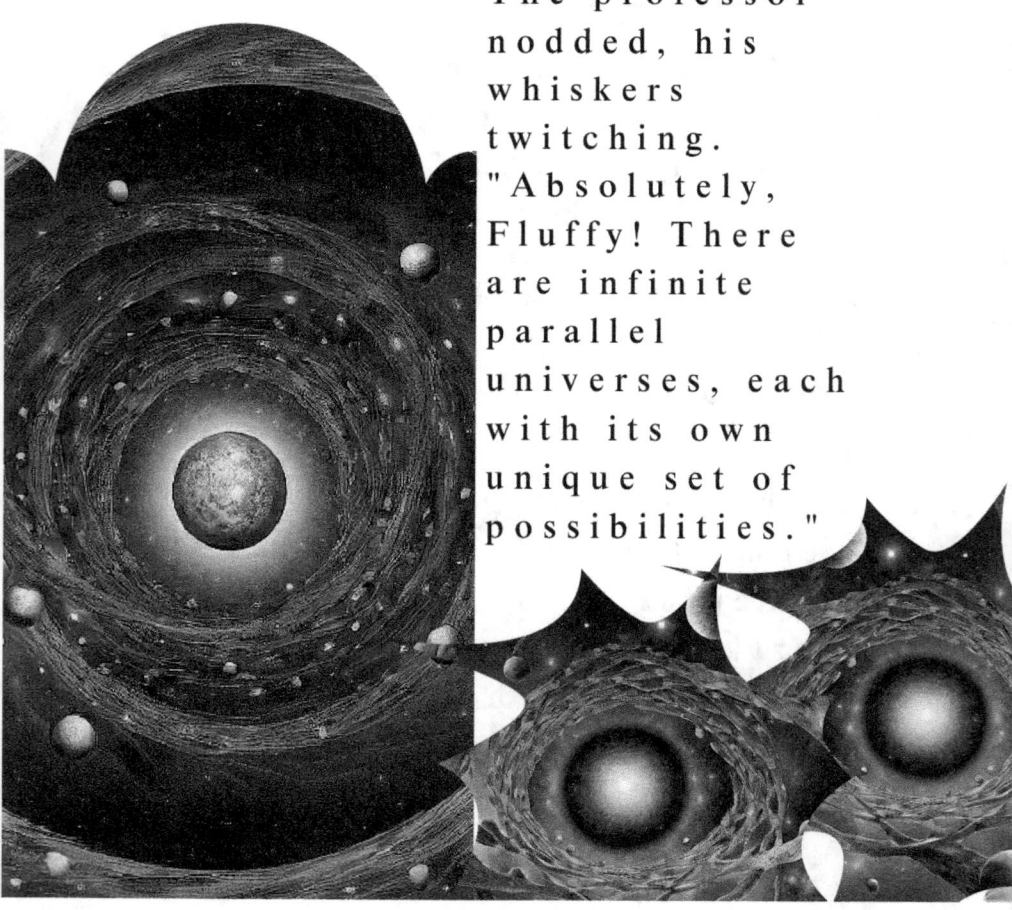

"Some may have different laws of physics, while others might have different species or even alternate versions of ourselves."

They even encountered a universe where time flowed backward; gravity was much more robust, and even a universe where everyone communicated through music.

They even played a "What If?" game where Fluffy would imagine a particular scenario, and Professor Whiskerborrow would explain how it might play out in a parallel universe.

This made learning about parallel universes a fun and interactive experience for Fluffy.

Finally, after traversing several parallel worlds, they stumbled upon a portal that shimmered with a familiar glow.

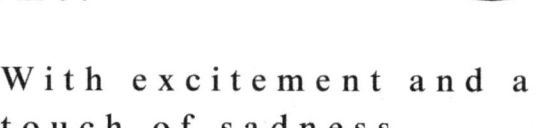

It was Fluffy's way back home!

With excitement and a touch of sadness, Fluffy bid farewell to Professor Whiskerborrow, knowing she would cherish their shared memories forever.

"Thank you, Professor Whiskerborrow, for showing me the wonders of the multiverse," Fluffy said, her voice filled with gratitude. "I will never forget our incredible adventure together!"

The professor
nodded, his eyes
gleaming with
pride.
"Farewell, dear
Fluffy.
Remember, the
universe is vast
and full of
infinite
possibilities.
Keep exploring,
and who knows
what other
adventures await
you."

Fluffy leaped through the portal
with one final purr and returned
to her familiar backyard.

She was home at last! And there
at the other end stood Dr.
Whiskerwilde, smiling a cheekish
smile.

"So it was you all the time, Dr
Whiskerwilde!"

It took her some time to let all
her experiences sink in.

From then on, she carried with her a newfound knowledge. Yet, she continued her mischievous escapades, spreading joy and curiosity wherever she went, secretly dreaming of the parallel universes she had visited and the friends she had made along the way.

Fluffy embraced each day with a sense of wonder.

SUPPLEMENTARY READING
5

Theory of the Quantum Multiverse

The theory of quantum multiverse, also known as the Many-Worlds Interpretation, is a fascinating concept in physics that suggests the existence of multiple parallel universes or alternate realities.

According to this theory, every time a quantum event occurs, such as measuring a particle's position or momentum, the universe branches off into different possibilities.

Each branch represents a different outcome, creating a separate reality.

Parallel universes exist separately from our own.

To understand this better, let's imagine a simple example. Imagine flipping a coin. In our world, the coin will either land on heads or tails.

However, in a quantum multiverse, the theory suggests that both outcomes occur in different multiverse branches.

So, in one branch, the coin lands on heads, and in another department, it lands on tails.

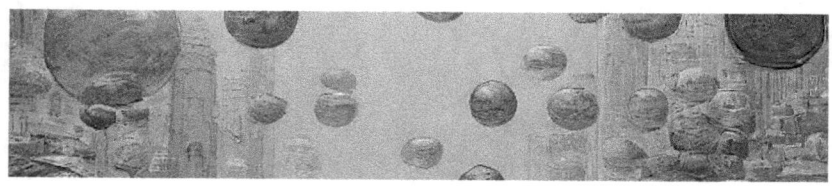

8

ENERGY CRISIS IN THE COSMIC CRYSTAL

Sparksville was becoming enchanting, all because of curious friends - Zoom, Zap, Photonix, and Quarky.

It was nestled in the heart of the Cosmic Realms, unlike any other town.

It was where quantum events and the mundane intertwined, creating a harmonious existence for its inhabitants.

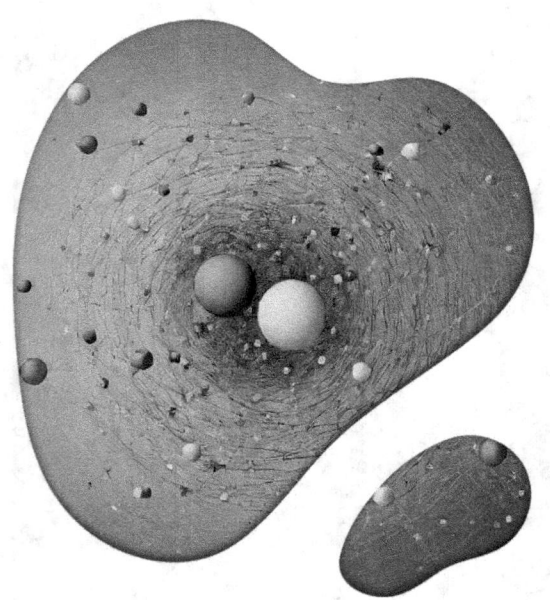

At the center of this mystical town stood the Cosmic Crystal, a magnificent jewel that radiated with the power of quantum energy.

Like everyone else in Sparksville, our friends Zoom, Zap, Photonix, and Quarky, who were inseparable, were among the few chosen beings in Sparksville who thrived on this quantum energy.

They possessed unique abilities, each harnessing a different aspect of the Quantum Realms.

Zoom had the power of speed, Zap could control electricity, Photonix could manipulate light, and Quarky could bend reality.

The friends spent their days exploring the wonders of Sparksville, using their powers for the greater good.

They helped repair broken
quantum gadgets, lit up the
town's darkest corners with
quantum radiance, and even
raced against time to avert
disaster. Together, they were the
protectors of Sparksville's
magic.

However, one
fateful day, the
friends noticed
a disturbing
change.

The Cosmic
Crystal, which
had always
glowed with an
otherworldly
brilliance, had
started to dim.

Its once
vibrant
energy was
waning,
causing the
magic in
Sparksville to
fade away.

The people of Sparksville   **100**
grew worried as the town began
to lose its enchanting charm.

Zap discovered it
first and
reported it to his
friends about it,
exclaiming, "Oh
no! The Quantum
Crystal is losing
its energy!

Without it, our
dear Sparksville
will gradually
lose its balance."

Quarky looked
very concerned as
she said, "We
need to find out
what's causing
this and how to
restore its energy.
The balance of
our realm depends
on it."

The other two friends nodded while sharing their concerns.

Photonix said, "I've heard that disturbances can influence the Cosmic Crystal's energy in the quantum realm. We must embark on a quest to investigate and restore harmony."

Zoom then suggested, "Let's use our knowledge of quantum principles to guide us. I remember reading about quantum fluctuations, where energy levels vary unpredictably."

As the friends set off on their quest, they ventured into the heart of the town, looking for clues.

Soon, their search bore fruit
as they encountered some strange
phenomena.

Objects flickered
in and out of
existence, and
reality seemed to
warp and shift.

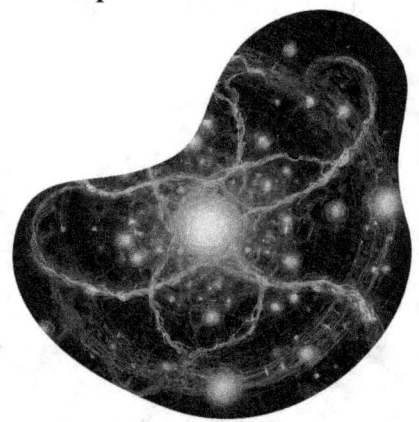

Zap exclaimed:
"Look!
Everything is
fluctuating.
It's like the
quantum
energy is
unstable."

Quarky chipped in with her know-
how: "I think the Void Essence is
causing these disturbances.
Perhaps the disturbances are
causing fluctuations in the
Crystal's energy."

Photonix chipped in: "Let's
investigate these disturbances
and try to restore stability. We
must find a way to bring balance
back."

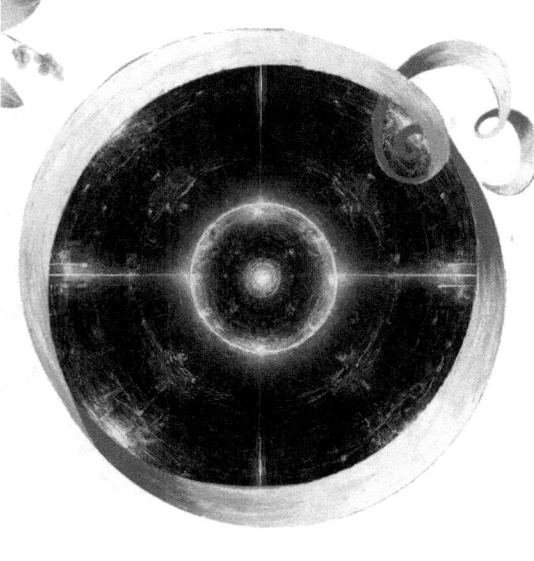

Zap exclaimed: "Great idea! Let's observe the patterns of the fluctuations and see if we can discern any clues."

The friends delved deeper into the issues, studying the patterns of the quantum fluctuations and how they could revert the forces of the Void Essence.

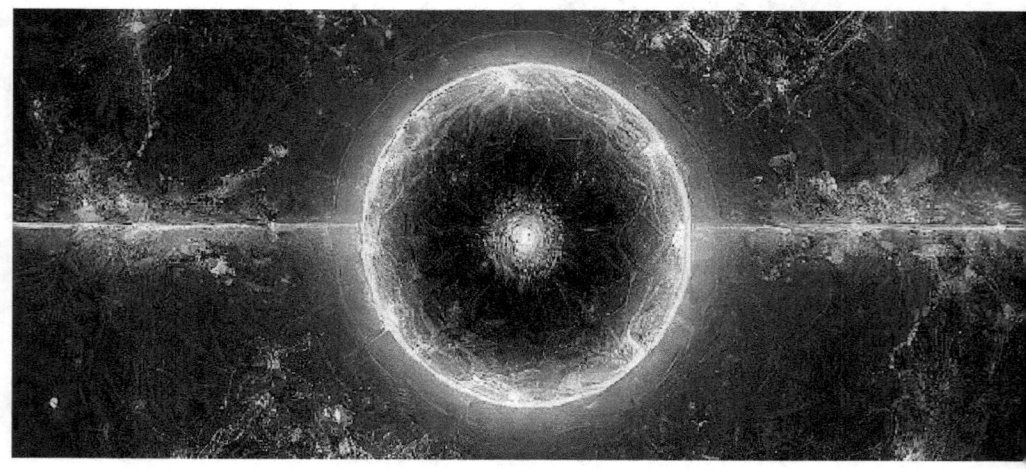

They noticed that certain areas emitted stronger disturbances than others. This was probably their clue.

Zoom said as he monitored the energy with a device, "These areas with stronger fluctuations might hold the key to restoring the Cosmic Crystal's energy."

Zap suggested, "Perhaps we can counteract the disturbances by introducing opposite energy patterns."

After considering it, Photonix said, "Let's use our intuition and experiment with different energy combinations to restore balance."

Zap was quick to support Photonix's suggestion, "Excellent plan! We must work together to harmonize the energies and stabilize the Cosmic Crystal."

Through their collaborative efforts and understanding of quantum principles, the friends managed to identify the specific disturbances causing the imbalance.

They carefully manipulated the energies, harmonizing them with the Cosmic Crystal's natural state.

Soon, they got their breakthrough, and Quarky exclaimed excitedly, "We did it! We've stabilized the Cosmic Crystal's energy."

Zoom responded with joy,
"Now, it can radiate its power
throughout Sparksville once
again, restoring balance and
harmony."

Photonix
cautioned,
"And let's
remember the
importance of
vigilance and
preventive
actions. We
must stay
attuned to any
future
disturbances to
maintain the
balance."

Zoom said in a tone of
profound realization,
"Once our journey
taught us that
understanding
quantum principles is
essential in upholding
the harmony of our
realm."

Quarky continued, "It's fascinating to think that. Quantum energy can be so intricate and delicate. Even small disturbances could significantly affect the Crystal's stability."

Indeed, this quest allowed them to learn more about the quantum realm and its complexities.

Thus, with the Cosmic Crystal's energy restored, Sparksville regained its balance.

The friends were hailed as **108**
heroes, and their quest became
legendary, reminding everyone of
the power of quantum energy and
the significance of maintaining
balance.

And so, the adventures of Zap,
Zoom, Phtonix, and Quarky lived
on, inspiring new generations to
explore the wonders of quantum
principles and protect the
delicate equilibrium of their own
realms.

SUPPLEMENTARY READING
6

Using Quantum Energy in the Real World

Using quantum energy in practical applications is an ongoing scientific research and exploration area. Harnessing quantum energy for everyday use is still in the early stages of development.

Some research areas include quantum computing, quantum cryptography, and quantum sensing.

Quantum computers, for one, rely on manipulating and utilizing quantum energy in the form of quantum bits or qubits.

9

JOURNEY IN A TIME CAPSULE

Once again, here in Sparksville, we are into another adventure involving our friends Zoom, Zap, Photonix, and Quarky.

They were the best of friends and loved exploring new things together. And this time, they are about to embark on a timeless adventure - so to say.

It so happened that one sunny afternoon, while playing in the park, they stumbled upon an old, dusty chest buried deep in the ground. Curiosity sparkled in their eyes as they pried open the chest to reveal a shiny, metallic object.

They examined it more closely and saw it had several distinct characteristics.

It was a time capsule!

The friends knew that time capsules are typically buried underground and contain items or information intended to be opened or accessed later.

Excitement filled the air as they wondered what secrets it held.

They eagerly opened the time capsule without wasting a moment and were instantly surrounded by a bright, glowing light.

When the light subsided, the friends found themselves in a world that looked both familiar and strange. Tall buildings reached for the sky, cars zipped around without making any noise, and people wore sleek gadgets on their wrists. It was the future!

As they walked along the bustling streets, a friendly voice echoed through the air.

"Welcome to the future, young explorers! I am Nebula, your guide to this amazing world," said a holographic figure appearing before them.

"Wow, this is incredible!" gasped Zap.

Nebula smiled. "Indeed, it is! In the future, quantum technology has revolutionized everything. Let me show you some marvels."

They followed Nebula to a transport station where a sleek pod awaited them.

"Hop in," Nebula said. The friends hesitated for a moment, but their curiosity overcame any fear. They stepped inside, and the pod whisked them away in an instant.

"Woah! We're moving so fast!" exclaimed Zoom.

"That's because this pod uses quantum propulsion," explained Nebula, even as the pod whizzed past buildings and landscapes.

"With the power of quantum propulsion, transportation has become incredibly fast and efficient," Nebula continued explaining, "But hold tight, we're about to take a quantum leap!"

The pod accelerated even faster, and the kids could feel the exhilarating rush as they zoomed through the cityscape, passing by skyscrapers that seemed to blur into streaks of color.

The pod accelerated even faster, and the kids could feel the exhilarating rush as they zoomed through the cityscape, passing by skyscrapers that seemed to blur into streaks of color.

"Whoa! This is like being on a roller coaster!" Zap exclaimed, gripping the sides of her seat.

As they zipped through the city, the pod suddenly tilted and soared into the sky. They could see the Earth below them, the clouds parting as they reached a breathtaking height.

The pod then came to a stop in front of a magnificent glass tower.

They stepped out and saw people conversing through small, translucent screens attached to their wrists.

"What are those?" asked Quarky.

"Those are quantum communicators," replied Nebula, "They use quantum entanglement to connect people across vast distances instantly. You can talk, see, and even share holographic images with just a flick of your wrist."

The four friends exchanged amazed glances. Photonix said, "Imagine talking to our friends back home with these!"

Quarky grinned and replied, "Yeah, we could have secret conversations without anyone even knowing!"

As they continued their journey, they marveled at the sight of floating drones gracefully gliding through the air, purifying it with their advanced quantum technology.

They watched in awe as these drones effortlessly removed pollutants, leaving behind a cleaner and fresher atmosphere.

Their exploration led them to a building that seemed to come alive before their eyes.

It was made of shimmering quantum materials that repaired them selves, healing any cracks or damages with a mesmerizing dance of particles.

The friends couldn't help but touch the walls, amazed by the magic of self-repairing structures.

And just around the corner, they stumbled upon a bustling restaurant where a robotic chef with quantum supercomputers prepared delectable meals in seconds.

They marveled as ingredients transformed before their eyes, combining and sizzling in perfect harmony.

The aroma filled the air, making their tummies rumble with hunger.

"I wish we had a chef like this at home!" Photonix exclaimed, licking his lips in anticipation.

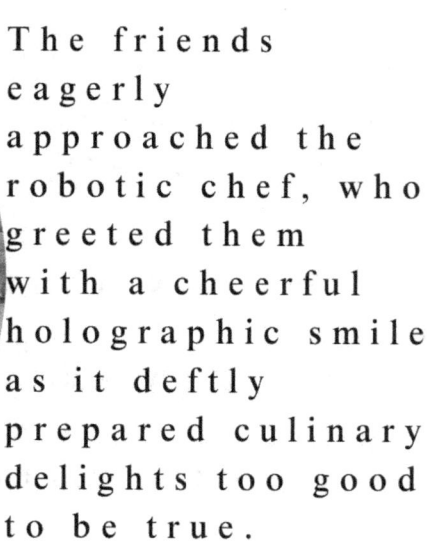

The friends eagerly approached the robotic chef, who greeted them with a cheerful holographic smile as it deftly prepared culinary delights too good to be true.

"Would you like to try our **120**
quantum-infused cuisine?" the
chef asked, displaying an array
of mouthwatering dishes.

Quarky's
eyes widened
as she
pointed to a
plate of
chocolate
chip cookies
that
appeared
magically
before her.
"I'll take
those,
please!"

With their appetites satisfied and
hearts filled with wonder, the
four friends bid farewell to the
futuristic restaurant, their minds
buzzing with excitement about
the limitless possibilities of
quantum technology.

Eventually, **121** they reached a grand library filled with books, but instead of paper, they noticed shimmering holographic screens displaying endless knowledge.

"This is the Quantum Library," Nebula announced. "Quantum computers have enabled us to store vast amounts of information and access it instantly. It's a treasure trove of knowledge!"

Amidst their awe, Zoom asked, "How can we bring these advancements to our time?"

Nebula smiled.
"By nurturing your
 curiosity and love
 for learning, you
can become the
scientists,
engineers, and
inventors of the
future. Quantum
science holds

incredible potential, waiting to
be discovered by minds like
yours."

With newfound
inspiration and
a mixture of
excitement and
sadness, the
young explorers bid farewell to
Nebula and the marvels of the
future.

They stood
before the
time capsule,
their eyes
fixed on its
gleaming
surface.

Remembering the
stories they had
heard about the
power of belief
and imagination,
they closed their
eyes and reached deep within
themselves.

As they visualized their own
time, the familiar streets of
Sparksville, their friends'
laughter, and their families'
warmth, a surge of energy pulsed
through the air.

 As the familiar
park came into
view, they couldn't
wait to share their
incredible
adventure
with their friends
and families.

The time capsule responded to
their collective will, its hum
growing stronger and brighter.

In a flash of light, the young explorers felt themselves being pulled, as if by invisible hands, through the fabric of time itself.

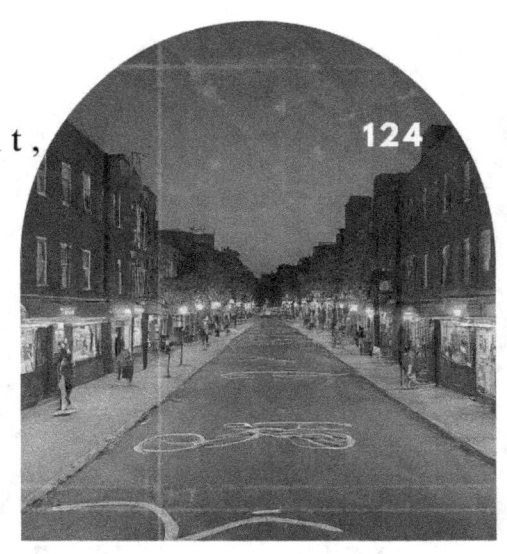

They were enveloped in a swirling vortex where past, present, and future intertwined.

And just as quickly as it had begun, the whirlwind of time subsided.

Our friends stood once again in the park, surrounded by the comforting embrace of their own time.

The time capsule stood before them, silently witnessing their incredible journey.

They realized that their voyage to the future had been more than just a fantastical adventure - it had instilled within them the power to imagine, dream, and shape the world around them.

And so, the young explorers returned to their own time, but with hearts full of wonder and minds brimming with dreams of the future they could create.

With hearts brimming with gratitude and minds teeming with possibilities, Zap, Zoom, Photonix and Quarky they walked away from the time capsule, forever carrying the wonders of the quantum realm in their souls.

10

THE QUANTUM ZOO

Our four friends, Zap, Zoom, Photonix, and Quarky, decided to play a prank on the residents of the classical world in classical time realms. They chose our time on planet Earth!

Back in time and home on planet Earth, a group of friends, Max, Sarah, and Ben, were visiting the Zoo when they saw something amazing.

"Look!" Max said. "That rabbit is in two places at once!"

The other two friends looked where Max was pointing. Sure enough, the rabbit was sitting in its cage, but it was also standing in the corner of the cage.

"That's impossible," Sarah said.

"How can a rabbit be in two places at once?"

"It happens in a quantum world," Ben said. "At the quantum level, things can be in two places at once. It's called superposition."

"That's so cool!" Max said. "I wish I could be in two places at once."

"Me too," Sarah said. "But I'd probably get lost."

The friends continued to watch the rabbit, fascinated by its quantum behavior. Suddenly, the rabbit disappeared.

"I don't know," Sarah said. "But it's not the only one."

The other animals in the zoo were starting to disappear, too.

"What's happening?" Ben asked.

"I don't know," Sarah said. "But we have to find out."

The friends started to investigate. They talked to the zookeeper, but he didn't know anything. They searched the zoo, but they couldn't find the missing animals.

Finally, they found a clue. In one of the cages, they found a piece of paper with a message written on it.

"We've taken your quantum animals, and they are kept in a secret room," the message said. "If you want to see them again, you must solve our riddle."

This was the handiwork of our four friends from Sparksville!

The riddle was a puzzle about the quantum world.

So read the riddle, "A cat is in a box. The cat is both alive and dead at the same time. If you open the box, the wave function will collapse, and the cat will either be alive or dead. But until you open the box, you don't know which one."

Our Earthly friends knew that this riddle was based on the concept of superposition in quantum mechanics.

Superposition is the idea that objects can be in two states at the simultaneously.

In the case of the cat, the cat is both alive and dead simultaneously.

When you open the box, you collapse the wave function, and the cat becomes either alive or dead.

The riddle is a way of introducing the kids to the strange and counterintuitive nature of quantum mechanics. It's also a way of getting them to think about the role of observation in the quantum world.

The riddle is a challenging one, but it's also a thought-provoking one.

It's a way of getting our kids to think about the nature of reality and the role of observation in the quantum world.

On reading the note, Sarah asked, perplexed, "What does that mean, 'the cat is both alive and dead'?"

Max replied, "It means the cat is in a superposition state. It's both alive and dead at the same instant."

Sarah exclaimed. "That's impossible!"

Max replied, "It's not   **133**
impossible. It's how things and
events in the quantum worlds
work."

Sarah tried to probe further,
"But how can something be two
things at the same time?"

Ben chipped in, "I don't know
how to explain it. It's just one of
those things that you have to
accept."

Sarah was
adamant, "But I
don't want to
accept it!"

Ben replied,
"Well, you don't
have to. But you
do have to
understand it."

The kids realized this was the
same principle used to hide the
animals at the zoo.

The animals were all in a state of superposition, which meant they could be anywhere, both in the zoo and not in the zoo.

The kids figured out that the only way to find the animals was to collapse the wave function.

This meant that they had to find a way to interact with the secret room in a way that would cause it to become either real or not real.

The kids started by looking for clues.

They looked for anything that might give them a hint as to where the secret room was located.

They looked for strange symbols, hidden passages, and anything else that seemed out of place.

After a while, the kids started to find some clues. They found a strange symbol carved into a tree.

The strange symbol carved into a tree was a quantum entanglement symbol.

The strange symbol carved into a tree was a quantum entanglement symbol.

The kids knew that quantum entanglement is a phenomenon where two objects are linked together in such a way that they share the same fate. This meant that if the kids could find the other half of the symbol, they could find the secret room.

They soon came to a waterfall. There was a hidden passage behind the waterfall. The kids knew that waterfalls are often used as symbols of transition.

This meant the hidden passage behind the waterfall was likely a portal to another world. The kids followed the path and eventually found the secret room.

The kids followed the clues and eventually found the secret room. It was a room that was filled with quantum-related objects.

"At least now we know where the animals are!" Max said

Now, they had to open the box. This meant they had to find the secret room where the animals were being held.

The friends went to the place where the animals were being held.

They found the animals in a secret room. The kids had solved the riddle and found the whereabouts of the animals.

Once the kids found the secret room, they opened the door and collapsed the wave function. This caused the animals to either be alive or dead. The kids were relieved to see that the animals were all alive.

They could collapse the wave function by interacting with the room in a way that caused it to become real.

Max put it this way, "The secret room was in a state of superposition. We had to find ways to interact with it."

The animals were all in superposition, just like the rabbit had been. The friends used their knowledge of quantum mechanics to free the animals.

The animals were so grateful that they gave their friends a special gift.

"This is for helping us," the animals said. "It's a quantum amulet."

The animals were actually our friends from Sparksville!

The quantum amulet was a small silver necklace.

The Earthy friends could see the world differently when they put it on.

They could see the quantum behavior of all the objects around them.

The friends were so excited about their new gift. They knew that they would never forget their adventure at the Quantum Zoo.

As they walked away from the Quantum Zoo, they knew that their adventure had not only gifted them with unforgettable memories but also ignited an everlasting passion for the quantum realm.

With the quantum amulet in their possession, the kids could invoke the quantum realms whenever they wanted to and be protected in their adventurous sojourns through the different kingdoms.

Amil Imani

Welcome to the enthralling world of quantum possibilities! Within the pages of this book, you will embark on a journey of scientific wonders and mind-bending concepts that will stretch the limits of your imagination.

From the eerie superposition of objects existing simultaneously in multiple states to the perplexing phenomenon of quantum entanglement, these short stories offer glimpses into the enigmatic realm of quantum mechanics. Each tale encapsulates the essence of this captivating field, presenting you with characters who grapple with its intricacies and face extraordinary circumstances.

As the author, I have sought to blend scientific accuracy with the thrill of storytelling, immersing you in the strange and fascinating world of the quantum. These tales aim to ignite your curiosity and leave you pondering the profound implications of quantum phenomena on our perception of reality.

www.ingramcontent.com/pod-product-compliance
Lightning Source LLC
Chambersburg PA
CBHW061247170626
46809CB00007B/2889

* 9 7 8 0 9 8 3 6 9 0 9 2 4 *